CONNIE S. ARNOLD

MUDCAT THE PIRATE

THE ADVENTURES OF RA-ME
THE TRAVELING TROUBADOUR BOOK 3

Mudcat the Pirate
THE ADVENTURES OF RA-ME THE TRAVELING TROUBADOUR BOOK 3

Copyright © 2019 Connie S. Arnold.

iUniverse books may be ordered through booksellers or by contacting:

iUniverse
1663 Liberty Drive
Bloomington, IN 47403
www.iuniverse.com
1-800-Authors (1-800-288-4677)

ISBN: 978-1-5320-7393-9 (hc)
ISBN: 978-1-5320-7391-5 (sc)
ISBN: 978-1-5320-7392-2 (e)

Library of Congress Control Number: 2019904597

Print information available on the last page.

iUniverse rev. date: 04/18/2019

iUniverse®

Dedicated to my husband, who is my most loyal supporter! Love you.

"You say it's my turn, Falstaff? O. K., I'll begin. Once upon a time... Oh, I sure hope it will happen only once. And, I really did see Mudcat the Pirate disappear before my very eyes. Just went up in smoke!"

Falstaff and I are boon companions. But for those of you who don't know me, my name is Ra-me—you know as in do-re-mi-fa-so-la-ti-do. I am a freelance minstrel and a traveling troubadour. The things that have happened to me!

"Ah, I know, Falstaff, I'm wandering from my story. Yes, it's a new one. Of course, it's true; I know that skeptical look of yours."

After my successful gig at the castle in Parkingham, and after my concert at Dragon Village to help young Blaze get his fire back, I was feeling pretty proud of myself. I was ready for my next gig.

Well, when the next invitation came, it seemed pretty tame. It came from Fair Haven Village on the shore of Lake Fairhaven. I was invited to perform at the christening of a new sailing vessel called the *Good Ship Lightning Bolt*. The largest body of water I had ever seen was the moat around Parkingham Castle. But *Lake Fairhaven*, on which the *Good Ship Lightning Bolt* would sail, was huge, almost an ocean. Along the coastlines are many mysterious caves and hidden coves covered by jungle-like overhangs. I had heard that some of these caves had unexplored depths.

Sometimes the surface is like a mirror, a blue, quiet reflection of the sky. Occasionally, strong winds churn the lake, throwing up violent waves filled with debris from the lake's belly.

Part of the celebration was to be a parade, so I took my piccolo as well as my lute. I polished my instruments, packed my sailor blouse and bell-bottom trousers, saddled my mule, Roscoe, and started my journey. Roscoe was wearing a new saddle, his tail decorated to make him look like a seahorse.

As I rode, I wrote poems for sailors. I made them rollicking and bouncy like a ride on a ship. I set them to music and practiced my songs as I went along.

The invitation in my pocket read:

> RA-ME, TROUBADOUR, AND SINGER OF ALL SONGS, IS HEREBY MOST CORDIALLY INVITED TO PERFORM AT THE CHRISTENING OF THE *GOOD SHIP LIGHTNING BOLT* ON LAKE FAIRHAVEN. YOU WILL RECEIVE A BAG OF GOLD FOR YOUR APPEARANCE.
>
> MERRILYN, THE MERMAID, WILL DO THE HONORS OF BREAKING A BOTTLE OF SPARKLING WATER ON THE BOW.
>
> HOPEFULLY YOURS,
>
> **CAPTAIN SKIP JACK**
> SKIPPER JACK WAV-ER-LEE
> CAPTAIN OF THE GOOD SHIP LIGHTNING BOLT

Every time I read the note, my heart skipped a beat. A mermaid. An honest-to-Pete mermaid. I had heard of them, but I didn't know they were real. Now I was to see one. I could hardly wait. This seemed like an easy way to earn a bag of gold.

The road that leads to Fair Haven Village was well-traveled, so the ground was smooth and hard. Others traveled on the way with us to attend the christening and the festival to be held on *Lake Fairhaven's* banks.

When I finally arrived, I immediately knew something was wrong. From a distance, everything looked all right; but as I got closer, I could see that the tents were faded and the banners were torn. Very few pies, cakes or tarts were offered for sale. The pig roasting on the

spit was very thin, no juices dripped from his skinny frame. The apple in his mouth was shriveled. The people attending the stalls were colorfully dressed, but there were patches on their clothing, and all the villagers were thin. It didn't take long for the people traveling the road with me to buy up all the offered wares. I was glad that I had packed some food in Roscoe's saddle bags.

But the fun went on as though nothing was amiss. Games were set up on the green: horseshoes, ring toss, apple bobbing. Admirers had set up stands where they could watch and cheer their favorites in the footraces! There were games that I didn't recognize.

But there, moored at the pier, was the vessel to be christened! She gleamed white with her name painted in gold on her side: *Good Ship Lightning Bolt*. Her brass was polished and blazed golden in the sun.

"Ah, Ra-me, glad you found us," Captain Skip Jack shouted.

His uniform was bright blue, accented with two rows of burnished brass buttons marching down the front. Gold epaulets were perched on each shoulder, white gloves tucked under his belt. His beard was neatly trimmed, except for his long fuzzy sideburns. His smile was toothy and white in his sun-tanned face.

"And this is our festival queen, Miss Lulu Belle," he introduced. "She will be in the parade tonight. You will lead, of course, playing on your piccolo, and Lulu Belle will walk directly behind you. She will be waving at the crowd, throwing flowers and candy. What fun!

He rubbed his hands together, smiling from ear to ear. Captain Skip Jack was just a young man, looking forward to a fun event. He didn't say anything about Merrilyn, the mermaid, who, I supposed, was waiting at her home in the lake.

"Lulu Belle was beautiful, and she was smiling right at me. Of course, Falstaff, you know my face turned red." I bent over the hand that she offered me.

"Shall we walk?" she invited. "There is much to see."

"We walked over the entire green. I wanted to ask her why the village was so poor, but I thought that would be impolite. She walked on the ground. But, Falstaff, I felt like I was walking on air above the ground! I listened to her every word. And, Falstaff, I even grew brave enough to buy a seashell bracelet for her tiny wrist."

The afternoon passed too quickly, and it was time to dress for the parade.

Splendid in my sailor's suit, I was mounted on Roscoe at the head of the parade. Festival Queen Lulu Belle walked closely behind us, followed by crowds of village people costumed in sea-going themes: sailors, pirates, Neptunes, fish masks. Lulu Belle was dressed as a pirate's lady and threw flowers into the crowds that lined the sides of the parade route. The laughter and cheering rang throughout the night. A considerable bonfire threw light all around.

The next morning the crowd was still in a happy mood. They gathered at the waters' edge for the christening ceremony.

"Ladies and gentlemen," Captain Skip Jack shouted through a polished brass megaphone. "Ra-me, the troubadour, will now play for us while we wait for our shy guest to appear." I knew he was talking about Merrilyn, the mermaid. My lips quivered in such excitement that I could hardly pucker to play my piccolo.

Soon, out in the harbor, a tiny ripple widened into a circle in the waters' surface, and her head appeared. "Ah, Falstaff! She was a vision to behold: golden hair entwined with ribbons of seaweed; green eyes lustrous in her smooth, pale face; strawberry lips in a cupid's bow." She

balanced on her mermaid tail and lifted her hands to receive the bottle of sparkling water that Captain Skip Jack held at the waters' edge.

Gracefully, she swung the glass bottle at the ship's bow as Captain Skip Jack said, "I christen you *Good Ship Lightning Bolt!*" The bottle made contact with the ship. But, alas, it didn't break.

Merrylin's laughter was the sound of tinkling bells as she dived back into the water, waving to the crowd, unaware of the unbroken bottle. Her tail glimmered as if it were encrusted with jewels of many colors.

"A curse! A curse!" the crowd shouted. When the bottle doesn't break, a curse is put upon the ship. Toasting and naming a vessel must be shared with Neptune. He must have his part of the drink!

Captain Skip Jack, having retrieved the bottle, opened it and poured half of the contents into the water and half on the hull of the boat. Maybe this would appease Neptune, and he would allow them smooth sailing on his lake. Just perhaps, the curse would only amount to a bad case of stomach bug. Quickly, licorice was handed out to the crew members. This was supposed to ward off stomach ailments.

But suddenly, low-hanging clouds appeared over the celebration, shrouding all in darkness. Thunder roared, accompanied by torrents of rain. Then another ship appeared, without warning, in the harbor right beside the *Good Ship Lightning Bolt.* Its dark hulk looked the same size and built on the same lines, which would make it a swift-moving vessel. Its sails, half-billowed in the wind, made the white skull and crossbones shine brightly in the darkness. A streak of lightning allowed me to just make out the name on its side, *Pirate's Revenge.* Its black lettering was edged in gold.

"Mudcat the Pirate!" Frightened cries echoed in the stormy sky. The heavens were still leaden, but a tiny light was beginning to grow on the horizon. Suddenly, the wind filled the sails of the pirate ship flaunting the jolly roger, and it sped off under the dark clouds toward the sun in the distance. As Mudcat steered his boat out to sea, the darkness lifted.

The sun revealed a crowd huddled and frightened on the docks around the harbor. Captain Skip Jack was calming the crowd. "I'm certain that Neptune is now appeased. I can protect us from Mudcat the Pirate with my new fast ship!"

I was standing at the end of the gangplank, holding tightly to Roscoe's halter. As I started walking further on the boardwalk, I spied an object on the boards. It was the bracelet that I had bought for the Festival Princess, Miss Lulu Belle. The little seashells were still fastened on the bracelet, but the clasp was broken. I looked around for her, but she wasn't anywhere in the crowd.

"Captain Skip Jack, Captain Skip Jack," I called to him.

"Troubadour, what is it?" he asked.

"Miss Lulu Belle is missing. I found her broken bracelet."

"Oh, no," he exclaimed. "It's that pirate; he has taken her!"

"Are you sure?" I asked.

"I'm sure. Mudcat kidnapped my brother a year ago! And he warned us we'd be sorry if we didn't invite him to the festival. I must go after her."

"Yes, you must," I agreed.

"And you must come with me," he said.

Startled, I asked, "Me? Why?"

"Aren't you the troubadour, singer of all songs? You have to sing a song that will persuade him to give her back," he said.

"Now, Falstaff, I would have gladly given up any gold I might be offered, but the Festival Princess must be rescued. Maybe the Captain wouldn't really need my help, so, I stopped protesting. I held tightly to Roscoe's lead rope as the Captain pulled us both onto the ship, and we set sail."

The storm still raged above our ship, and we were rocking on the rolling waves. I hung my head over the rail, and I'm ashamed to say that I lost everything I had eaten that day. Roscoe's head was beside mine over the railing, too. His cry was pitiful to hear!

Soon, the curse lifted, and the winds blew the clouds away; it was now smooth sailing on *Lake Fairhaven*. No longer seasick, I could stand and look outward. In the distance, I could see the Pirate's Revenge. The winds now billowed us full sail, and we were bounding toward the other vessel. But as I watched, the pirate's ship disappeared behind a huge rock.

"No," shouted Captain Skip Jack. "He can't get away this time!"

"Where did he go?" I asked.

"I don't know. Perhaps into one of the many hidden coves, I guess. But we must capture him. The village is poor because Mudcat steals all the goods that our people send out for sale to other ports. Everyone has worked on the *Good Ship Lightning Bolt* to make it fast enough to catch the pirate ship. It's all up to us, Troubadour, to save the village and its people and rescue Lulu Belle. We must find him, and you must sing him a siren's song. A siren's song will lure him into doing whatever you ask."

"Now, Falstaff, I knew what a siren's song was supposed to do, but I am no enchanter. But the pirate had all the gold! It really belonged to the villagers, and I knew I wouldn't get even a small bag of it if this pirate weren't caught."

"Aye, aye, Captain. What's the plan?" I agreed. My salute was awkward.

We sailed up and down the coastline to see what we could spy. After we discovered nothing, we found a smooth place to tie up at waters' edge. Then Roscoe and I followed the Captain down the gangplank onto the shore.

"I'll leave my crew on board, and you and I will walk the shorelines looking for a trail into a hidden cave."

I secured Roscoe to a tree, and the Captain and I started out. As the trail branched off in two directions, we parted company. When I was out of the Captain's sight, I played little trills on my piccolo. Its music vibrated through the open trees.

Suddenly, the piccolo trill hit a wall and echoed back to me. There was something hidden in the thicket of trees just off of my trail. I left the path and found a stack of cut saplings blocking an entrance to a cave. Cautiously, I crept forward.

There in the middle of the cave before a small campfire stood Mudcat the Pirate. He had black hair held back with string, a bushy black beard, and a black patch over his left eye. A wooden peg leg was strapped at his knee. He must have sent his crew members and Lulu Belle away, because he was alone. He looked sad.

I began to play on my lute the most haunting melody I could conjure up. He looked up at me with tears in his eyes. I sang of a man caught in a web of sorrow, doing things that he didn't really want to do. I sang of a man who tried to make things right, and a man who wanted to go back to his family. "Really, Falstaff, the words just poured out of me. I sang of a story that I couldn't have known. Now, Mudcat was really crying!"

Then it happened. Mudcat the Pirate disappeared before my eyes. He pulled off the wig, the beard, and the eye patch and put them on the fire. Next, he unstrapped the peg leg, revealing a healthy limb. The wooden leg went into the fire. He shed his pirate's costume, and Mudcat the Pirate went up in smoke. Underneath, he wore the clothes of a villager.

The pirate's clothes burned quickly, and puffs of black smoke sped upward, bringing Captain Skip Jack running into the cave.

"What's this?" he asked. He looked at the man in astonishment. "My brother!" He ran to the man, and no bear could have given the man a bigger hug.

"Your brother?" I asked.

"Yes, this is Jacob. The night that my brother disappeared, Mudcat the Pirate left a note bragging about kidnapping him and stealing my fastest ship. He, also, kidnapped two of my brother's friends. Jacob and I had had a fight that night, so I have regretted not being able to say I was sorry. Jacob, how did you get away?"

"Mudcat let me go. He knew that your new ship would be fast enough to catch him. He dropped us here and sailed away. He said we would never see him again."

"Now, Falstaff, this story was beginning to make some sense. When he ran away from home, Brother Jacob had become Mudcat the Pirate. My song had reminded him of how homesick he really was. So, Jacob had scuttled the pirate ship, and now he had to make Mudcat disappear."

"What about Lulu Belle and your two friends?" asked Captain Skip Jack.

"All safe," Jacob answered.

"And, Falstaff, they were safe. We found them in a nearby cave, tied up, and seated comfortably on blankets. And, Falstaff, all the loot that had been pirated from the villagers had been sold. The gold that Mudcat had gotten for it filled three big bags. The village wouldn't be poor anymore!"

"But, Jacob," Skip Jack protested. "Mudcat didn't take the gold?"

"No. I told him how strong and brave my big brother is, and that he had better leave before you came," Jacob said. "Jack, can I come home? I'm sorry, too."

"Of course, you can come home. I don't even remember what caused us to fight!"

"Falstaff, there was another big bear hug. We loaded our passengers and the gold onto the newly-christened *Good Ship Lightning Bolt* and sailed home under a clear sky. The villagers lined the shore, waving handkerchiefs in greeting."

The villagers held another festival. This time they were dressed in new clothes, the tents stood sturdy and tall, the banners above the stalls were bright, and tantalizing aromas wafted from the many pies, tarts, and goodies to tickle our noses and make our mouths water. The pig roasting on a spit was fat, and juices dripped from the meat. The apple in his mouth was rosy and round.

Lulu Belle was still the Festival Queen, but she and Jacob walked arm in arm, leading the parade. Nothing was more important than the forgiveness of the brothers, tying the family back together. Jacob was to join Captain Skip Jack in sailing and selling the villagers' wares to other ports, so all was forgotten.

I was paid my bag of gold, and I played gaily on my piccolo as I rode Roscoe back toward home. My sailor's suit was safely packed in Roscoe's saddlebag. I hoped that I would never again be called upon to sail when the waves were tossing.

"Mudcat, the Pirate, would forever remain a secret shared only by Jacob and me. Well, and you, too, Falstaff. But you must never tell anyone, ever."

Printed in the United States
By Bookmasters